What Can I Be?

DISCARD

Written by Cari Meister
Illustrated by Matt Phillips

Children's Press®
A Division of Scholastic Inc.
New York • Toronto • London • Auckland • Sydney
Mexico City • New Delhi • Hong Kong
Danbury, Connecticut

For Simon and Corrina
—C.M.

To Mrs. Phillips, the best teacher
in the whole world
—M.P.

Reading Consultants

Linda Cornwell
Literacy Specialist

Katharine A. Kane
Education Consultant
(Retired, San Diego County Office of Education
and San Diego State University)

Library of Congress Cataloging-in-Publication Data

Meister, Cari.
  What can I be? / written by Cari Meister ; illustrated by Matt
Phillips.
        p. cm. — (Rookie reader)
Summary: A young girl wonders what she can be as she tries on
different costumes from her dress-up box, and finds that being
herself is the best choice.
  ISBN 0-516-22876-5 (lib. bdg.)   0-516-27810-X (pbk.)
  [1. Identity—Fiction. 2. Individuality—Fiction. 3. Costume—Fiction.
4. Stories in rhyme.] I. Phillips, Matt, ill. II. Title. III. Series.
  PZ8.3.M5514Wh 2003
  [E]–dc21
                                        2002015596

CHILDREN'S PRESS, and A ROOKIE READER®, and associated logos are
trademarks and or registered trademarks of Scholastic Library Publishing.
SCHOLASTIC and associated logos are trademarks and or registered
trademarks of Scholastic Inc.
8 9 10 11 R 12 11 10   62

What can I be?

Too scary.

Too hairy.

Too silly.

9

Too frilly.

11

Too green.

Too mean!

Too hot.

Too many spots!

What can I be?

I can be me!

Word List (15 words)

be	hot	scary
can	I	silly
frilly	many	spots
green	me	too
hairy	mean	what

About the Author

Cari Meister lives on a small farm in Minnesota with her husband John, her sons Edwin, Benjamin, and Aaron, their dog Samson, two horses, three cats, two pigs, and two goats. She is the author of more than twenty books for children, including *I Love Rocks*, *Game Day*, and *A New Roof* in the *A Rookie Reader* series.

About the Illustrator

Matt Phillips has been doodling since he could hold his dad's fountain pen without poking himself. He's been happily drawing ever since. Sometimes he stops to play the mandolin or banjo or squeak away on the fiddle, but he pretty much draws all the time. He has a wonderful wife who teaches school, and two dogs that don't teach anything. He also has a cat that likes to knock over his ink and ruin final art with her inky footprints. His doodles can be found in books, magazines, malls, greeting cards, websites, advertisements, and little wadded up piles all around his drawing table. He lives and works in White, Georgia.